NEW BEGINNING
and Home Away from Home

NEW BEGINNING
and Home Away from Home

Rachel Starr

authorHOUSE®

AuthorHouse™ LLC
1663 Liberty Drive
Bloomington, IN 47403
www.authorhouse.com
Phone: 1-800-839-8640

Published by AuthorHouse   08/22/2013

ISBN: 978-1-4918-1116-0 (sc)
ISBN: 978-1-4918-1117-7 (e)

Any people depicted in stock imagery provided by Thinkstock are models, and such images are being used for illustrative purposes only.
Certain stock imagery © Thinkstock.

This book is printed on acid-free paper.

Because of the dynamic nature of the Internet, any web addresses or links contained in this book may have changed since publication and may no longer be valid. The views expressed in this work are solely those of the author and do not necessarily reflect the views of the publisher, and the publisher hereby disclaims any responsibility for them.

Dear Readers

If you need encouragement or someone you know needs encouragement this should help with explaining the 23rd Psalm better

The Lord is my Shepherd: Jehovah—Rohi God my Shepherd:

Jesus said, "I am the Good Shepherd who knows my sheep by name. The Lord of the universe knows you personally! Thank Him for your relationship with Him.

Pray for others:

Jesus is the Great Shepherd of all his sheep. Pray for someone who is discouraged and thinks God has forgotten them. Pray for them to know God is their shepherd.

I shall lack nothing: Jehovah—Jireh: The Lord my Provider:

If God provided so much in Jesus to meet your Spiritual needs, will He not also take care of your daily practical needs? Pray, Give us this day our daily bread, and name the specific needs you trust Him for. Thank Him he is your Provider.

Pray for Others:

Pray for those who have real financial needs and for those who are discontent with what they have.

He makes me lie down in Green pastures. He leads me beside quiet waters:

Jehovah—Shalom: God is Peace:

Pray about anything that is disquieting your peace. Affirm that God is your peace. Pray about God's leading in His work in your life and your decisions.

Pray for Others:

Ask God how to pray for someone in a hard place. Pray for Him to calm all your fears, worry, doubt, anxiety with the Prince of Peace in their heart.

He restores my Soul: Jehovah—Rapha:

Where do you need healing and restoration of Jesus the Healer?

Pray for Others:

Pray for God to heal the hurts, bitterness, control, judgments, differences, separation, wrong priorities etc. of someone you know.

He guides me in paths of righteousness: Jehovah—Tsidkenu: The Lord my righteousness:

Pray for God's guidance as you dedicate yourself to follow Him as Lord.

Pray for someone else:

Jesus declares us to be righteous, for what we have done, but because of His perfect righteousness. Pray for Salvation for someone who not received Jesus as God's perfect sacrifice for their sins.

For His namesake: Jehovah-m'kaddesh:

God's name is Holy. He says "I am the Lord alone am holy, and I make you holy because you are called by my holy name. Pray that you will not dishonor His name.

Pray for Others:

Pray that someone away from God will desire to bring glory and honor to His name.

Even though I walk through the valley of death, I will fear no evil for you: Jehovah-Shammah:

God is there. Jesus promised His disciples, I have all authority; I am always there for you. Affirm His presence with you that dispel fear and unbelief.

Pray for Others:

God promised His presence in Exodus 3:12 for leading the children of Israel out of Egypt. In Exodus 33:14 reaffirms His presence to finish want He began. Ask God to reveal himself to your friends and family in powerful new way.

Your rod and your staff, they comfort me:

You can depend on the rod of His protection and correction of your Good Shepherd.

Pray for Others:

His comfort is as warm and tender as that of a mother for her child. Who needs you to pray for them?

You prepare a table before me in the presence of my enemies: Jehovah—Nissi:

The Lord my Banner **of Victory:**

Praise God that He gives victory over your enemies and sins, as you depend on the authority of your crucified, resurrected Victorious Redeemer.

Pray for Others:

Pray the same prayer for your friends and family.

You anoint my head with oil:

Oil is used for medicine, Sanctification and signs of friendship. Oil symbolizes the Holy Spirit who is all things. Thank God for the power of the Holy Spirit to heal, restore, soothe cleanse and give a sign of your fellowship with the Father and His Son.

Pray for Others:

Pray that your family and friends will live in the Spirit.

My cup overflows:

Exercise you attitude and gratitude.

Pray for Others:

Pray that your family and friends will praise God continually as their source.

Surely goodness and love will follow me all the days of my life:

Thank God for specific evidence of His goodness and love, He has shown you daily.

Pray for Others:

Thank God for people who has shown His goodness and love to you? Pray that they will see God's goodness in them.

And dwell in the house of the Lord forever:

Ask God to show you how to practice, His presence, with you continually.

Pray for Others:

Ask God for the body of Christ to worship Him with their whole heart and be committed to the living in His Presence daily.

God Bless,
Rachel Starr

A NEW BEGINNING

MAIN CHARACTERS

David Spencer   —   the local vet and a born again
                             Christian

Danielle Spencer   —   David's wife

Danny Spencer   —   David and Danielle's son

Debby Spencer   —   David and Danielle's daughter
                             who has Down syndrome

Robert Jackson   —   a back slidden Christian who
                             turned away from God

Robin Jackson   —   Robert's deceased wife who died
                             shortly after giving birth to their
                             daughter

Rebecca Jackson   —   Robert and Robin's daughter

Pastor Joe Brown   —   minister of the local Church

Carrie Brown   —   Pastor Joe's wife

Hope Curtis   —   Robert's future wife

Barbara (Bobbi) Curtis —   Hope's daughter

The entire bible verses used in this book is taken from The New
International Version

PROLOGUE

Phoenix 1985

ROBERT AND ROBIN WERE childhood sweethearts. After college Robert and Robin got married. It was a beautiful wedding. A few months later Robin was pregnant with their first child. A few months into her pregnancy she was diagnosed with Pre-eclampsia this was caused by high blood pressure.

Robin had fallen in the last months of her pregnancy; the doctor told her that she was fine. Shortly after the birth Robin had a Cerebral Hemorrhage that occurred during the fall and was never treated. As a result Robin died shortly after giving birth to their daughter Rebecca.

A NEW BEGINNING

A small town in Iowa 1998

DAVID SPENCER AND HIS family lived in a big two story house. David was the local vet. With being the local vet he would get calls at all hours of the day and night. There had been times when he would often miss church.

He knew this was nothing that could be helped; his family understood that his work came first.

David's wife Danielle and their son Danny gave riding lessons for the local children in the surrounding areas.

Robert and his daughter lived in a big farm house with several barns for horses and other farm animals. Robert and Rebecca had only brought Rebecca's horse Cinnamon with them, but after being here a short time he had to go to a horse auction to get more horses for breeding purposes. Robert was a freelance writer. Robert had taken writing classes in college. He had gotten a job as the editor of the college newspaper. He wrote about the upcoming school dances and football games. After the games he put the scores and who won in the local newspaper.

After college he got a job writing articles for the local newspaper and magazines. After Robin's death he asked to do all his work at home so he could be there for his daughter Rebecca.

David had gotten a call from Robert. Rebecca's horse had not been eating and has been lying on the floor not moving. When David arrived David said, "You must be new in the area, I haven't seen you in town."

Robert said, "We just moved here a few weeks ago." Robert continued, "Did you find anything wrong with Cinnamon, this is my daughters horse and she would be heartbroken if anything happened to her."

David asked, "Has Cinnamon been eating?" Robert said, "She was eating before we moved here, but not since we been here."

David told Robert, "I believe I found the trouble, I was checking her over and I felt some type of blockage in the abdominal area."

David said, "We need to clean her out, with a hose and lots of warm water. What have you been feeding her?"

Robert said, She was eating hay and the grass in the pasture over there."

David said, "That shouldn't have caused the problem. Where did you come from before moving here?"

Robert told him, "We lived in Phoenix, and with living in the city we had to board Cinnamon at a stable in the country."

David made the comment, "That could be it, I'm not sure, but since Arizona is drier than here maybe the chemicals that they use when they plant, might be different than what we use."

David asked, "How did you get here? I assume you didn't fly since you brought a horse with you?"

Robert said, "We drove here, I wanted to fly but Rebecca wanted to take her horse. I told her we could get her another horse when we got here. But Rebecca wouldn't listen."

David said, "We are having a bible study at our house tonight, why don't you and your wife come? The bible study is open for whoever wants to come. You can bring Rebecca along she would be a good companion for our daughter Debby. Debby was born with Down syndrome. Debby is 13, how old is your daughter,"

"She is 13," Robert told him. As for my wife, she died 13 years ago. She died of a cerebral hemorrhage shortly after Rebecca was born."

David said, "I'm sorry, we will be praying for you and your daughter."

Robert asked, "I have heard of children with Down syndrome. Can you tell me a little more about it? I am a freelance writer for the local paper and I would like to do a story about Debby if that would be alright?" David said, "That would be fine, Debby will be excited. Nothing like this has ever happened to her before."

Robert said, "I'm sorry for the interruption, you were talking about a bible study. We don't go to church anymore. God and I don't talk." David made the comment, "Robert, God always talk to us, and we just don't always hear Him."

"If ever you need someone to talk to I'm a good listener and Pastor Joe has an open door policy. The church doors are always open and anyone can come in and pray any time day or night."

Robert said, "Thanks but no thanks."

After David left Robert was very quiet he went to his room, he kept a picture of Robin on the dresser.

Robert was thinking, Robin why did you have to die, I miss you so much. Robert just sat on the bed and started to cry.

Later that night Rebecca asked, "Did Dr. Spencer come out to take of Cinnamon?"

Robert had a lot on his mind and wasn't listening.

Rebecca said, "Daddy did you hear me." Robert looked at her, "What did you ask me?"

Rebecca said, "Did Dr. Spencer come out and take care of Cinnamon?"

Robert responded, "Yes he did and Cinnamon is fine."

Rebecca asked, "What is Dr. Spencer like, is he nice?" Robert said, "I suppose he is we don't know much about him though. All I know is that he is a Christian and he was having a bible study at his house tonight."

Robert continued, "I wanted to tell him what he could do with his mumbo jumbo."

Rebecca said, "Daddy, you didn't say that did you!" Robert said, "No, I didn't but I thought about it."

Rebecca said, "I would like to go the bible study I want to learn more about Jesus. When we lived in Phoenix my friend Samantha and I would talk about Jesus."

Robert asked, "Why didn't you tell me you were doing that?" Rebecca said, "I didn't want to tell you because I was afraid that you would be upset and you would yell at me." Rebecca was close to tears. Rebecca said, "Why do you yell at me all the time? I know that you blame me for mom's death, but you shouldn't take it out on me. I wish you would love me like a dad should love his child." Rebecca was crying now.

Robert said, "We are both very upset and we will discuss this later. Right now I am tired and I'm going to bed."

Robert knew that Rebecca was right; he shouldn't blame her for her mother's death it was something that just happened. Robert loved Rebecca and he knew they didn't talk much, he just didn't know how to tell her.

David and Danielle had the bible study, Danielle asked, "David did you talk to Robert about the bible study?" David said, "I did but he said ever since his wife died he didn't want anything to do with God."

"One of the neighbor ladies asked, 'Did he say how his wife died?' David said his wife died shortly after giving birth to their daughter of a cerebral hemorrhage."

The neighbor said, "Oh my! We definitely have to pray for that young man and his daughter." David said, "I told him about Pastor Joe and the open door at the church. He told me, "Thanks but no thanks." After that I left.

Debby said, "Dad can I pray for him and his daughter?" David looked at her, "yes honey you may." Debby closed her eyes and prayed.

"Dear Jesus, I want to bring Robert and his daughter to you right now. Please give them the strength to go on day by day. I know you love them and care about them. I pray in time they will come back to you and start living a Christian life again. Amen."

The group followed suit, "Amen." David said, "That was lovely sweetheart. I hope you and Rebecca will be friends. Rebecca is also 13."

Danielle said, "Maybe I should go over there and see if they need help. I'm sure that it might be hard for a 13 year old to grow up without a mother. She might need a mother figure to maybe talk about things a mother would talk daughter about."

David said, "That would be a good idea, but I think that you should wait a little while though." Danielle said, "Maybe your right."

Robert called David to ask when he could come over to interview Debby. David said, "Any time would be fine."

A couple days later Robert came over. Robert said, "Debby I would like to ask you if anyone comes in to help you with exercises or anything." Debby said, "Yes, I have an occupational therapist that comes on Monday, Wednesday, and Friday. The physical therapist comes on Tuesday and Thursday." Robert asked, "What do the therapists do you for you?" Debby said, "The occupational therapist helps me with maintaining my daily living needs, like hygiene. Sometimes I have difficulty with my fine motor control and she helps me with my hand exercises. The physical therapist works with my gross motor skills so I can participate in family activities." Robert asked, "Is there anything else?"

Debby said, "If mom doesn't have time for cooking, then my occupational therapist helps me with cooking. She is teaching me new recipes, also she helps with other things too so in time when I'm older I will be able to live in my own apartment."

Robert said, "Thank you very much Debby, I will type this up and send it to the different papers."

A couple of weeks later Robert had told Rebecca that she could go to the bible study but she had to find her own way to get to David's house. Robert continued, "I am not taking you because David would invite me in and I would feel obligated to stay. I am not ready to have someone to preach to me and that includes you Rebecca."

Rebecca said, "How do you expect me to do that." Robert said, "I don't know. Call them to pick you up."

Rebecca called, "David, this is Rebecca Jackson; I would like to come to the bible study. Could you come and pick me up?"

David answered, "Yes, I will be there in a few minutes." Rebecca said, "Thank you, bye,"

When David arrived, he introduced himself. Hi Rebecca, my name is David."

Rebecca said, "Hi, it's very nice to meet you, I wanted to thank you for taking care of Cinnamon." David said, "You're Welcome. I am very glad that you decided to come, your dad said you never go to church."

Rebecca said, "We don't but I told dad that I wanted to come because when we lived in Phoenix, my friend Samantha and I talked about Jesus and I wanted to learn more about Jesus."

David asked Rebecca, "If you ask your dad maybe you can go to church with us, we will be happy to pick you up."

Rebecca said, "I would like to go with you. I will ask dad when I get home tonight." David said, "My daughter is 13, she was born with Down syndrome. Our son Danny is 16 he is going to be going to be going to college after high school. He told me he wants to become a vet like me."

David continued, "Here we are, everyone I would like you all to meet Rebecca." Everyone said, "Hi Rebecca." Danielle said, "I'm Danielle, David's wife, this is our daughter Debby, this is our son Danny."

Pastor Joe said, "I'm Pastor Joe and this is my wife Carrie." Everyone else introduced themselves.

After the bible study Danielle asked Rebecca, "David told us about your family; if there is anything I can do just let me know. I know that it must be hard for you being raised without a mother, I'm sure you there are things you would like to tell a woman that you can't talk to your dad about, just let me know." Rebecca said, "I will, thank you Danielle."

When Rebecca got home she was very excited about getting to know more about Jesus. Robert said, "I see your home." Rebecca said, "Yes, and David wanted me to ask you if I could go to church with them. David said they would pick me up. Also Danielle told me that if there was anything I wanted to talk about she would listen."

Robert said, "Who is Danielle?" Rebecca told him, "Danielle is David's wife. Debby and Danny are their children." Robert asked, "What kind of things does Danielle want to talk about?" Rebecca said, "Things like shopping for clothes, teaching me how to cook, things that a mother would talk to her daughter about."

Robert said, "Why would she do that, she's not your mother?" Rebecca said, "I know but she wants to be like a mother, since I don't have a mother."

Robert said, "Are you going to remind me that you don't have a mother? I know you don't have a mother. I just think she shouldn't be butting into our business."

Rebecca responded, "Danielle is not doing that, she just thought that you wouldn't want to take me shopping and talk about girl stuff."

Robert said, "She's right, I don't, but you just met her and it's like she is taking over as a parent."

Robert continued, "I want to meet Danielle but I don't want to discuss any church stuff."

Rebecca said, "I can call her and ask her to come over." Robert said, "That's fine, I want to talk to her." When Danielle came over she also brought Debby with her. Danielle said she was going to take Debby clothes shopping after their talk and maybe Rebecca would be able to come too.

Robert asked, "Why do you want to do things with Rebecca?" Danielle said, "as I told Rebecca I want to tell her things that a mother would talk to her daughter about. Rebecca is a little young yet but in time she's going want to talk about boys and dating and things like that. I would love to be that person to talk to her about that. I will be talking to Debby too."

Robert said, "I never thought about that kind of stuff." Rebecca went with Danielle and Debby shopping, Danielle bought Rebecca and Debby new clothes for school; they also went to the horse supply store to get new riding clothes, which included boots, shirts and a cowboy hat. After shopping the girls went out for lunch.

After lunch Danielle took Rebecca home. When Rebecca got in the house she showed her dad what Danielle bought her? The next day was Sunday, David and his family picked Rebecca up for church.

Pastor Joe said, "Hi Rebecca, it is so nice to meet you again. Do you remember my wife, Carrie?

Rebecca said, "Yes I do, how you are today?" Pastor Joe and Carrie said, "We are doing just fine today."

Pastor Joe had done a fine sermon, Rebecca really enjoyed it. While the Spencer family took Rebecca home, Danny asked, "Debby and I are going riding in the woods near our house tomorrow, would you like to join us?"

Rebecca said, "Yes I would love that, what time should I ride over?" Danny told her what time. That way you can stay for lunch, alright."

Rebecca said Alright, see you tomorrow."

Debby said, "You can ride with us anytime you want to, just come over. You don't need to call first, right dad?" David said, "Right come anytime."

Rebecca continued to go to church and the bible studies every week. Rebecca rode Cinnamon over for the bible studies. The Spencer's picked her up for church.

As Rebecca cleaned the house and did the dishes she was singing and praising God as she worked. Robert was in his office working and was listening to his daughter sing. Robert remembered how Robin had loved to sing all over the house.

While Robert was listening to Rebecca sing, he saw a woman the woman who looked like Robin. Robert said, "Robin is that really you?" Robin said, "Yes it's me, I came because I have a message for you. I want you to start believing in God again, you need to start living in the present not in the past. You need to find someone to love again; I want you to know that I'm fine I never intended to leave you; I want you to start living a Christian life. I will never forget you and I will always love you."

Robert said, "I will never forget you and you will always be my first love." Robin said," Good bye, Robert."

Robert was crying he turned to get a Kleenex, and when he looked up Robin was gone. Robert said, "Robin come back, don't leave me again."

Rebecca was in the kitchen when she heard her dad talking; she assumed he was on the phone. She went to her dad's study. Rebecca asked, "Are you alright, you're crying." Robert said, "Come here sweetheart." Rebecca asked, "What wrong, you never call me sweetheart. Robert said, "I know, please come here." Rebecca came over; Robert gave Rebecca a big hug. Robert continued, "I just saw your mother, I thought I was dreaming. Your mother told me that I need to find someone to love again, and start going to church again."

Rebecca asked, "Do you want me to call David and have him come over so you can talk?"

Robert said, "No, not right now, I need to do some soul searching on my own and pray."

Rebecca said, "Ok, dad, I will be pray for you just like I always have." Robert said, "Thanks honey, good night." "Good night daddy." Rebecca came over and kissed Robert on the cheek.

Robert sat at his desk and started to pray. "Jesus, please forgive me for blaming you for Robin's death. Help me to be a better father to Rebecca. In many ways I blamed her too. If it will be your will help me to find the perfect mate. I know that I am one of your lost sheep, and you are the shepherd and you have been looking for me for many years. Here I am Lord, you found me, and I want to be part of your fold again. In Jesus name I pray Amen."

When Robert was done praying, he had tears in his eyes. Then he heard a voice, at first he wasn't sure what it was that he heard, then Robert remembered what David had told him about God always talks to you but we don't always listen.

Robert said, "I'm here God, I'm listening." The voice said, "Robert, I love you and will never leave you." Robert said, "I love you and I will never leave you."

After a couple of days of praying, Robert called David, to come over. David said, Is this a social visit or business? Do I need to bring my doctor bag?" Robert said, "No, just bring your bible and your wife if she would like to come with you."

David was intrigued, "Can you tell me what this is about?" Robert said," No, I will explain when you get here."

When David and Danielle arrived, David noticed something was different about Robert but he wasn't sure what it was.

Robert said, "Please have a seat in the living room, I will be there in a few minutes." David and Danielle sat on the couch and made small talk about how lovely the living room was decorated. Robert came in and said, "Thank you for coming over at the last minute." Robert continued, "A couple of days ago I was sitting in my office writing, I thought I saw someone standing in the doorway, I thought it was Rebecca. I looked and it was my wife Robin. Robin told me that she had a message for me. She said that I needed to start living again and start living a Christian life and start going to church."

David asked, "Did she tell you anything else?" Robert said, "Yes, she also said that she didn't want me to be alone. I know I have Rebecca, but she won't be with me forever." Robert continued, "Rebecca and I had a long talk, I wasn't being the father that I should be. That might not have been my exact words but she said she forgave me."

David said, "Congratulations Robert, now you are no longer a lost sheep." David continued, "May I pray with you now?" Robert nodded.

David prayed, "Lord Thank you for Robert, give him the strength and guidance that he needs to continue in his journey that you have set out for him. In Jesus name I pray, Amen. "Robert and Danielle both said Amen."

Robert mentioned, "I haven't been able to find any bible verses in the bible that I could read to help me in my journey."

David said, "I have some verses in mind that will help you, the first one is very simple.

John: 3:16

For God so loved the world that he gave his one and only son that whoever believes in him shall not perish but have eternal life.

Luke 19:9-10

9: Jesus said, to him, today Salvation has come to this house because this man too is the son of Abraham.

10: For this son of man came to seek and to save what was lost.

Revelations 3:20

Here I am, I stand at the door and knock. If anyone hears my voice and opens the door, I will eat with him and he with me.

Psalm 51:10-12

10: Create in me a pure heart O God, and renew a steadfast spirit in me.

11: Do not cast from me your presence or take your Holy Spirit from me.

12: Restore unto me the joy of your Salvation and grant me a willing spirit to sustain me.

David had written the bible verses down so Robert could read them later when he was alone. Robert asked, "Now, that I have rededicated my life to God. Rebecca and I would like to be baptized; can you ask the pastor if he will be willing to do that for us?"

David said, "Pastor Joe will do that but first Pastor Joe will need you to go to a class, in this class Pastor Joe will share bible verses on baptism and what it means to be baptized, and what it means to be born again."

Robert and Rebecca went to the baptism classes. Pastor Joe shared these verses.

Mark 16:16

Whoever believes and is baptized will be saved, but whoever does not believe will be condemned.

Acts 2:38

Peter replied, "Repent and be baptized, every one of you, in the name of Jesus Christ for the forgiveness of sins, and you will receive the gift of the Holy Spirit.

Pastor Joe said, "Accepting Jesus into your heart is only part of salvation. You need to be baptized in water than you will be filled with the Holy Spirit."

The next Sunday after church the congregation met at the lake not far from the church. Pastor Joe baptized Robert and Rebecca. Pastor Joe said, "Robert and Rebecca I baptize you in the name of the Father Son and Holy Spirit."

After the baptism everyone was invited back to the church for sandwiches and coffee and milk for the children.

Summer was almost over and Robert had gone to the school to register Rebecca for school. Rebecca said, "This is going to be so different." Robert asked, "Why do you say that?" Rebecca responded, "I wish Debby didn't have to go to a different school she is the only true friend I have here. I wish Samantha was here too." Robert said, "You will be fine, you will make friends fast.

Robert had planned to surprise Rebecca; he had been talking to Samantha's parents asking them if Samantha could come for a visit over Christmas vacation.

Robert had taken Rebecca to school on the first day, making sure she knew where all her classes were and to meet her teachers. Mrs. Curtis was one of Rebecca's teachers. Her husband had died in a skiing accident. She loved children, so that is why she became a teacher. Hope had one child Barbara, but everyone called her Bobbi. Bobbi was 11, but her birthday was coming up in a few weeks.

Mrs. Curtis said, "Welcome to junior high Rebecca, I'm sure you will make friends quickly." Rebecca said, "Thank you Mrs. Curtis, I'm sure I will."

Robert said, "I have to go; I will be here after school to pick you up. Meet me by the main doors where we came in."

Rebecca said, "OK, I will Bye daddy." Robert said, "Bye sweetheart." When Robert got home, he couldn't concentrate on his work. He kept wondering on how Rebecca was doing in school.

Robert had thought that Mrs. Curtis was very pretty; he also thought that her husband was a very lucky man to have had someone as special as Mrs. Curtis.

After school Robert went to pick up Rebecca. Robert was curious as to how Rebecca's day went. Robert asked, "How was your day?" Rebecca said, "I love school, I had lunch with Carol, she was very nice. She told me that she just moved here from Chicago. I told her we just moved here too.

Robert asked, "Did you make any other friends?" Rebecca said, "Not really, this is only the first day, so I'm sure I will make friends quickly just as Mrs. Curtis said.

Robert asked, "Do you like Mrs. Curtis?" Rebecca said, "Yes, I like her a lot. Robert said, "That's good, I thought she was very nice too."

When Robert and Rebecca got home, Rebecca asked, "May I go over to Debby's and tells her about school?" Robert said, "Yes you may." When she got there David told her that Debby wasn't home yet but she should be should be home soon.

David asked, "How do you like school?" Rebecca told David about her first day of school and about her new friend Carol.

David said, "I saw Mr. Hanson in town today. He worked at a big corporation in Chicago and he was transferred here." Rebecca asked, "Did Mr. Hanson say what he did in Chicago?" David said, "He didn't say."

Debby was just getting home and Rebecca and Debby went to her room and listened to records and ate a snack that Debby's mom brought them.

Rebecca had told Debby about the new friend that she met at lunch today. Debby asked, "Do you think she would like to come over sometime and we could go riding?"

Rebecca said, "I'm not sure but I will ask her tomorrow at lunch." Rebecca continued, "My teacher is really nice, her name is Mrs. Curtis. She has a daughter Barbara but everyone calls her Bobbi." Debby said, "That's a boy's name I never heard of a girl named Bobbi before." Rebecca said, "Neither have I, I will ask Mrs. Curtis if Bobbi can ride with us sometime too."

The next day Rebecca asked Carol if she wanted to go horseback riding with her and my friend Debby." Carol said, "I never went riding before, I'm afraid I will fall off." Rebecca said "Debby's brother Danny will be there, he trains horses and gives riding lessons." Carol said, "I'm not sure. I need to ask my parents."

Rebecca said, "That's fine, just let me know. I am going to ask Mrs. Curtis if her daughter can come. A few days later Rebecca, Debby, Danny, Carol and Bobbi went horseback riding in the woods. Carol said, "I've never been on a horse before, this was fun. I hope we can do this again soon." Carol said, "I am going to ask dad if I can have my own horse than I can come out here every day to ride."

That night after her homework was done Rebecca e-mailed her friend Samantha. Rebecca wrote that she missed her and that she made new friends. "Debby and her brother are our neighbors, and Carol is in my class". Samantha e-mailed back, "I miss you too. I just wish you didn't have to move away." Rebecca wrote So do I, but I like it here. At first I wasn't sure. Rebecca continued writing, "I almost forgot my dad and I accepted Christ as our personal savior." Samantha e-mailed back, "that's great. My family and I have been praying for you both." Rebecca e-mailed, "I have to go now, it's late and I have to get up early for school." Samantha e-mailed back, "Bye for now write back soon. Rebecca e-mailed back, "I will."

Thanksgiving was just around the corner, Robert and Rebecca didn't do much for the holidays because Robert felt that there was nothing to celebrate. This year was different; they had a lot to celebrate.

Robert mentioned, "Rebecca I think this year we should get a tree and put it next to the picture window." Rebecca said, "I think that is a good idea." Robert also mentioned, "David told me that they go into the woods by their house and he told me that we can go with them on Saturday." Rebecca said, "We have to buy ornaments we don't have any." Robert said, "I brought ours with us, the ones that mom and I put on our first tree as a married couple. I don't know why I brought them but now I know."

Rebecca said, "So do I dad, so do I." On Saturday Robert and Rebecca went over to the Spencer's farm and they found a big tree. As Robert was cutting down the tree he was thinking when he was going to tell Rebecca about Samantha's visit. He was thinking about the grandparents too. He thought they could come for Easter. Robert also was remembering his first Christmas with Robin and how happy they were.

Rebecca had a surprise for her dad. She contacted her grandparents (her dad's parents) and invited them there to surprise dad. Of course they accepted.

When they got home Robert got the ornaments down from the closet in the basement. As they both went through the boxes Rebecca noticed one that had a picture of her mom and dad on it and it said Our First Christmas.

Robert came over to see what Rebecca was looking at. Rebecca said, "Look at this one it as a picture of you and mom on the ornament." Robert said, "That was our first Christmas together as a married couple." Then Robert started to tear up. Rebecca asked, "Dad are you alright?" Robert said, "Yes, I was just remembering."

On Thanksgiving Day the Spencer family invited the Jackson family over for Thanksgiving dinner. Everyone went around the table and said what they were thankful for. After everyone had a turn David said the prayer.

Two weeks before Christmas Robert said, "I have a surprise for you," and Rebecca said, "I have a surprise for you too." They both said, "Samantha and Grandpa and Grandma Jackson are coming for a visit at the same time."

Robert and Rebecca looked at each other and started laughing and they hugged each other. A few days later Robert and Rebecca went to the airport and picked up Samantha and Robert's parents.

Robert's parents and Samantha were laughing when Robert told them what each of them did by surprising each other. When Robert's parents talked to Samantha's parents they had gotten on the same flight so Samantha would not have to fly alone. Samantha was glad she didn't have to fly alone.

She wasn't afraid because knew that God would be with her the whole way. Rebecca asked if she could take Samantha over to Debby's house to visit. Robert said, "Why don't you wait. I'm sure Samantha is tired from the trip."

Samantha said, "I don't mind Mr. Jackson, Rebecca told me all about her friends here. I would like to meet them." Robert said, "Alright but don't stay too long. I'm sure your grandparents would like to visit with you too."

Rebecca asked, "O.K, which horse can Samantha ride?" Robert said, "She can ride Snickers."

Samantha said, "Snickers why did you name him that?" Rebecca said, "We named him that because he is the color of Snickers candy bar and he has a birthmark on his forehead the shape of a peanut."

As the girls rode to Debby's house they talked about how they missed each other. Samantha asked, "What is there to do here in the winter?" Rebecca said, "I'm not sure, we could make a snowman. We can also hitch the horses to the sleigh for a sleigh ride. Samantha said, "I would like that."

Rebecca said, "There is a big shopping mall in the next town. Maybe we can talk to dad in taking us shopping. Grandpa and Grandma can come too."

When the girls got to Debby's house, Danielle told them that Debby was sick with a cold. Danielle said, "Why don't you have some hot chocolate before you go out again. You can still go riding if you want too. Debby should be fine in a day or two. With Debby's immune system she gets sick a lot easier than most people." Rebecca said, "I almost forgot where my manners are, this is my friend Samantha." Danielle said, "Hi Samantha, it's nice to meet you." Samantha said, "It's nice to meet you too Mrs. Spencer." "Please call me Danielle, everyone else does." Danielle said.

David had walked into house after taking care of a sick cow. Danielle said, "This is my husband David. This is Rebecca's friend from Phoenix." David said, "Hi Samantha, it's very nice to meet you, Rebecca has told us all about you." Samantha said, "Thank you."

Rebecca said, "Thanks for the hot chocolate Danielle, it was very good." Danielle said, "You're Welcome, bye girls." Both girls called back, bye Danielle."

Rebecca and Samantha went riding the trails.

After their ride Rebecca and Samantha came home and went to Rebecca's room to listen to records and talk some more.

The next day Robert asked, "Who wants to go for a sleigh ride?" Rebecca and Samantha said,

"Yes." Rebecca said, "We were hoping for a ride while grandma and grandpa were here. Can I call to see if Debby can come since she was sick yesterday?"

Robert said, "Yes, but make sure that it's alright with Danielle, I don't want Debby to get sick again."

Grandma asked, "What wrong with Debby that she gets sick all the time." Rebecca said, "Debby was born with Down syndrome and her immune system always attacks her in the winter. That is what Danielle told me."

Rebecca said, "Debby can't go out yet, but Danny is coming with us." Everyone enjoyed the sleigh ride the girls started singing carols and everyone else joined them.

The next day Samantha and Rebecca went riding on the trails again. Rebecca didn't see the patch of ice and she lost her balance and Rebecca and Cinnamon went down. Samantha was so scared. Samantha said, "Are you alright?" Rebecca said, "I think so." Rebecca got up but Cinnamon didn't. Rebecca said, "Go back to the house and get David. He is a vet and he will know what to do."

Samantha said, "I will be right back." Samantha rode back as fast as she could. When she got to the house she was out of breath. David saw her coming and knew something was wrong because Rebecca wasn't with her.

David said, "Where's Rebecca?" Samantha said, "There was a patch of ice and Rebecca didn't see it. Rebecca and Cinnamon went down Rebecca got up but Cinnamon didn't."

David followed Samantha to where Rebecca was waiting.

David asked, "Rebecca are you alright?" Rebecca said, "Yes, but my arm hurts." David checked Rebecca's arm. David said, "I think it's broken but x-rays will need to be taken to make sure." David continued, "Now let's check on patient number two." David said, "Rebecca Cinnamon's leg is broken she is in a lot of pain. I won't be able to fix the leg. I will have to put her down."

Rebecca said, "No, please try and fix it." David said, "If it was a sprain than I could do something. But Cinnamon is too badly hurt. I have to put her down."

David took the girls back to his house, than he took them home.

Rebecca was crying when she walked into the house. Robert asked, "What's wrong?" Samantha said, "There was a patch of ice and Rebecca and Cinnamon went down. Rebecca broke her arm and Cinnamon broke her leg and David said that Cinnamon had to be put down." Robert said, "Honey I am so sorry. Let me look at your arm. We need to go to the doctor."

Robert continued, "Mom, dad why don't you stay here with Samantha. I don't know how long we will be. So if you get hungry just fix yourself something. We will eat when we get home." Mom said, "No we'll wait for you to get back,"

When they got to the doctor's office they took x-rays and set Rebecca's arm. The doctor said, "You were lucky Rebecca that was a nasty break." The doctor continued, "You have to wear the cast for at least 6-8 weeks." .

Robert and Rebecca came home. Grandma asked, "Rebecca how do you feel?" Rebecca said, "My arm really hurts, but I'm alright." Rebecca continued, "I have to wear this cast for 6-8 weeks." Grandma said, "Robert we made dinner but we waited with eating until you got back." Grandma continued, "Robert I need to talk to you privately."

Robert said, "What is it mom?" Robert's mom said, "David came by. While you were gone he buried Cinnamon. He didn't know if he should make a marker or not." Robert said, "Thanks for letting me know, I'll call him later."

After dinner Robert called David. Robert said, "Wait with the marker; I want to talk to Rebecca first. I don't know if that would be a constant reminder to see Cinnamon's name on a marker." David said, "That's fine just let me know. I buried Cinnamon near the big oak tree by the waterfall along the trail. I like to ride out there and sit by the tree and look over at the waterfall." Robert said, "I know the place. I go there myself to think, it is so peaceful and quiet to reflect on God's creation."

The next day Robert asked, "Who wants to go shopping? I am not big on shopping. I know two girls who love to shop."

Rebecca asked, "Can we invite Debby?" Robert said, "If it's O.K. with Danielle than its fine with me."

After a day of shopping Rebecca didn't realize how much shopping would make her so tired.

Robert said, "Why don't you and Samantha go to your room and listen to records or whatever girls your age do. I will call you when dinner is ready." Rebecca said, "O.K."

When dinner was ready, Robert said, "Girls dinner is ready." He didn't hear a response. He called again. After the second call he went to Rebecca's room. Robert looked in and smiled, both girls were sound asleep on the bed.

Robert came downstairs and said, "The girls are asleep so I guess we're on our own for dinner."

Christmas and New Years went by so fast. Grandma and Grandpa and Samantha had to go back home. At School Mrs. Curtis asked Rebecca, "What happened, how did you break your arm?"

Rebecca explained how the accident happened, and that she wanted to eventually get another horse.

Mrs. Curtis said, "I'm sorry Rebecca, I guess you didn't have a very good vacation." Rebecca said, "It was pretty good, my grandpa, grandma and my friend Samantha came from Phoenix. Mrs. Curtis said, "That was nice." Rebecca said, "This was kind of funny. I surprised dad with grandma and grandpa and dad surprised me with Samantha." Mrs. Curtis said, "What about your mom didn't she go with you to pick them up?"

Rebecca said, "No, she died of a Cerebral Hemorrhage shortly after I was born." Mrs. Curtis said, "I'm sorry, my husband died in a skiing accident five years ago, so Bobbi and I are alone too."

Mrs. Curtis continued, "It gets pretty lonely with no one to share your dreams with." Rebecca said, "I used to feel very lonely and unloved. My dad used to blame God and me for my mom's death." Mrs. Curtis asked, "What happened? Your dad and you are very close now."

Rebecca said, "My dad told me that he saw mom. He thought he was dreaming because he was working hard and he was seeing things. Dad told me that mom had told him that he shouldn't blame anyone for her death and he should start living in the present and plan for the future or something like that I don't remember."

Rebecca continued, "after that dad and I had a long talk and dad asked me for forgiveness. Then dad talked to David Spencer, our neighbor, and dad and I accepted Christ into our lives. Dad was a Christian before but he turned away from God when mom died."

Mrs. Curtis said, "I was angry with God too. I prayed for forgiveness but I don't go to church." Rebecca said, "You and Bobbi should come to our church, Pastor Joe is very nice and he would be willing to talk to you. I'm sure my dad would talk you too. Since you both went through the same thing losing a spouse."

Mrs. Curtis said, "Maybe I will just do that, I know that I need to talk to someone." Mrs. Curtis continued, "Bobbi doesn't know what I have been going through the past five years."

When Rebecca came home from school she told her dad about her day and everything that Mrs. Curtis had told her about her husband. Robert said, "I will talk to her anytime she wants to talk." Rebecca said, "I will tell her tomorrow." Dad, do you know where David buried Cinnamon?" Robert said, "Yes he told me." Rebecca asked, "Where?" Robert said, "By the big oak tree next to the waterfall, why do you ask?"

Rebecca said, "I was wondering because I want to go and say my good byes. I told Mrs. Curtis that eventually I wanted to get another horse, but not right now. For right now I will ride the other horses. In time I would like a quarter horse."

Robert asked, "Why a quarter horses they are very expensive, I don't know if we can afford a quarter horses, it costs a lot of money. Rebecca said, "I don't expect to get one now. I would like a quarter horses so I could compete in barrel races." I am going to my room to do my homework, call me when dinner is ready I'll help with setting the table." Robert said, "Go ahead I have work to do, I have an assignment that is due than I need to send it in so it gets in the paper in time."

Before getting down to work Robert called David to find out what a quarter horse would cost and where you could board a quarter horse. David asked, "Why do you want to know?" Robert said, "Rebecca told me she would like a quarter horse, she wants to compete in barrel racing.

David said, "I will ask around. I have connections with being a vet."

Robert said, "Thanks, I appreciate it." David said, "No problem." A few days later David called and told Robert that he found someone who raises quarter horses and what it would cost to own a quarter horse. Robert asked, "How much." David told him. I go out to his farm and take care of his horses. I told him that I had a friend who was thinking about buying a horse for his daughter. He told me he would give us a good deal as a favor to me."

Robert said, "I would like to surprise Rebecca for her birthday." David asked, "When is her birthday." Robert said She will be 14 in April." Robert continued, "How much would it cost to build an arena? I am surprised that the other family before us didn't have one." David said, "The family didn't have horses they raised cattle and sheep."

Robert couldn't believe that Rebecca's birthday was just around the corner. Rebecca's grandparents called Robert. "We would like to know what Rebecca would like for her birthday."

Robert said, "She wants a quarter horse, she wants to compete in shows. After talking a few more minutes both sets of grandparents agreed to help pay for the horse. Since Robert's parents came for Christmas, Robin's parents wanted to surprise Rebecca with coming for her birthday. Robert promised not to tell Rebecca.

A couple of days before Rebecca's birthday, David had agreed to pick up Robin's parents up at the airport. Rebecca opened her presents; from David and Danielle she got a new saddle. Rebecca looked surprised she said thanks but I have one. David said, "We thought you would like a new one since the one you have is one we gave you to use."

From Debby she had gotten a horse brush and from Danny she got a gift card from the local horse supply store. Robert handed Rebecca a card, "This is from grandma and grandpa Jackson, grandma and grandpa Smith and from your dear old dad." Rebecca said, "Dad you're not old."

Rebecca opened the card she read, "I hope you are enjoying all your presents. You will need them." It was signed, Sampson. Rebecca said, "Who's Sampson?" Robert said, "Sampson is your surprise, remember I told you I had a surprise but I wouldn't tell you."

Robert continued, "Shall we all go to the barn. When Rebecca walked into the barn she saw a beautiful black horse. Rebecca said, "Where did he come from, he wasn't here yesterday."

David said, "Your dad wanted to surprise you with a race horse. I kept him in my barn and I brought him over this morning when you were in school. Robert said, "Weren't you wondering why I told you not to go in the barn today?" Rebecca said, "I was wondering why I couldn't ride Snickers after school."

Rebecca couldn't believe what was happening; she didn't expect a quarter horse so soon. Rebecca said "I can't wait to ride Sampson and start barrel racing." Danny said, "I can help you practice with barrel jumping, you can practice at our house until your arena is built."

Danny continued, "When you're ready, I can sign you up for different shows." Rebecca said, "That would be great! I know that this type of riding is different than riding the trails. Is there an age limit for racing?" Danny said, "There are different shows for all age groups. You will go in the 12-17 age group."

Danny continued, "I know there are some shows coming up in Dubuque and Davenport that you have a very good chance of winning if you practice." Rebecca said, "I plan on doing just that."

Robert said, "That's enough talk, why don't we all go in and have cake and ice cream."

The next day Danny was showing Rebecca how to canter and jump over haystacks to start out with. Danny also told Rebecca how to sit the correct way on the horse, by leaning to one side when going around barrels and cones.

Danny said, "You are learning fast Rebecca" Rebecca said, "I want to get even better. I want to compete in the barrel races that are coming up in a few weeks." Danny said, "Keep doing what you're doing and you will be ready."

The next few weeks went by fast. Danny timed Rebecca in jumping hurdles and going around barrels. The day finally came Rebecca was excited and nervous at the same time. Rebecca told her dad and Danny how she was feeling. Her dad said, "You will be fine. Let's pray and ask God for guidance."

After praying Rebecca felt better. Rebecca said, "I will do my best. The majority of riders here have been competing for years. I know they are better riders than I am." When it was Rebecca's turn the announcer said, "We have a new entry this year. Let's give a round of applause for Rebecca Jackson. Good luck Rebecca."

Everyone had a turn and did their best. Everyone waited to hear the results. "The winner is of the top prize and trophy is Rebecca Jackson!"

The announcer continued, "Congratulations Rebecca, please come up and collect your trophy and your check." Rebecca couldn't believe she won! Robert and Danny came over and congratulated Rebecca.

Robert said, "We need to celebrate, we can have a party! Rebecca you can invite your friends from school." Robert continued, "Danny it would have been nice if your parents could have come."

Danny said, "I know, they had planned on coming but at the last minute dad had gotten an emergency call from one of the neighbors. I guess when you're the vet you have to put business before pleasure."

At the party everyone congratulated Rebecca again. Some asked, "What are you going to do with all that money?" Rebecca answered, "I want to put it in the bank and save it for college?"

Robert overheard Rebecca talking. Robert said, Rebecca you want to save it for college."

Rebecca said, "Yes." Robert said, "That's a good idea, we never talked about college." "I have thought about it, I just don't know what I want to go to school for yet, but I have plenty of time to decide." Rebecca told her dad.

Over the summer months, Rebecca competed in other shows; she didn't win all of them. Rebecca was happy for the other entries; she wanted other families to be happy of their children too.

When school began Rebecca started high school. She was very nervous all over again starting in a new school and making new friends, but she still had her old friend's too. Although Rebecca wasn't in Mrs. Curtis's class anymore she still kept in contact with her. Rebecca had hoped that Mrs. Curtis and her dad would get together and go on a date.

Rebecca noticed that her dad was lonely Rebecca knew she had to do something about it. That night after dinner Rebecca went into her dad's office. Rebecca asked, "Dad there is something I want to ask you."

Robert looked up and asked, "What is it that you want to ask me?"

Rebecca said, "I was wondering if you ever thought about getting married again."

Robert said, "What brought this on?" Rebecca said, "I noticed that you have been very lonely lately. I think you should go out and have some fun." Robert asked, "Do you have someone in mind that I should ask." Rebecca said, "Yes, I think you should ask Mrs. Curtis. I never brought it up before because I was in her class last year and I didn't want anyone calling me the teacher's pet."

Robert said, "Mrs. Curtis is very nice, but I thought I would never get married again. Maybe I will ask her out sometime." Rebecca couldn't believe it; she didn't think it would be that easy.

Robert had called Hope. Robert said, "Mrs. Curtis, This is Robert Jackson Rebecca's dad." Hope said, "Hello is there something I can do for you?" Robert said, "I was just wondering how you were doing." Hope said, "I'm fine." Robert continued, "I also called to say that, I would like to get to know you better. I was wondering if you would like to go out sometime." Hope said, "I agree I would like to get to know you better too. I wanted to ask you the same thing but I didn't know what to say." Robert said, "I think we should do something with the girls first, to break the ice."

Hope said, "That would be nice." Robert asked, "What kinds of things do you like to do?" Do you like to go horseback riding?" Hope said, "I do, but living in town I don't get to ride much. I am kind of out of shape." Robert said, "I ride as much as I can. As you know Rebecca lives and breathes horses. I can't get her to come in to go to bed." Robert continued, "Do you go to church." Rebecca and I can pick you and Bobbi up." Hope said, "We don't go to church anymore. I thought I would like to start going again." Robert said "Good, we will pick you up on Sunday morning around 10:30; Church starts at 11:00. After church we can go on a picnic. I will make some sandwiches and potato salad." Hope said, "That's fine, I will bring the drinks." Robert said, "That would be fine, see you Sunday. Bye for now." Hope said, "Bye."

After church they all went to the park. The girls went on a walk around then park. Robert and Hope talked. Hope said, "My husband and I went to church every week. I stopped going when my husband died." Robert said, "I was the same way. I stopped when Robin died.

When Rebecca was older, my parents and Robin's parents wanted to take her to church."

Hope asked, "Did they take her to church." Robert said, "No, I wanted her to stay home with me. Rebecca told me that, she and her friend went behind my back, and talked about Jesus. Rebecca was afraid to tell me, because she knew how I felt." Hope asked, "When did Rebecca tell you this?" Robert said, "When we moved here. I was not happy with her at the time, but I knew I shouldn't be angry with her."

Hope said, "What did you say to her?" I told her I was tired and we would talk about it later. A few days later I told her she could go to the bible study and church, but I wasn't going to take her. David Spencer the local vet and his family picked her up for church. Rebecca and their daughter Debby are best friends."

Friday night was a high school football game. Danny was playing, everyone went to the game. Since Robert wrote for the local paper, Robert had to write who won, also what the score was. Also how many people were there. Hope and Bobbi were in the stands. Hope wanted to surprise Robert. She hadn't planned on coming but since that Sunday, Robert and Hope had been spending a lot of time together.

That night Robert had been thinking about Hope. Robert spent some time praying and asking God for guidance. He also prayed, "Robin you are my first love and I will always love you. I wanted to tell you that I met someone I want to ask her to marry me if she will have me."

A few days later Robert prayed and asked God to give him the right words to say. Robert called Hope and asked her and Bobbi to come Friday night for dinner.

Hope asked, "Is there anything I can bring." Robert said, "No, just bring yourselves." Robert continued, "There's something I have I need to discuss with you." Hope asked, Can you tell me what it is that you want to discuss?" Robert said, "No, I will talk about it on Friday." After dinner on Friday Robert asked everyone to come into the living room and have a seat. Hope asked, "Robert, what are you up to. You are being very mysterious."

Robert said, "Rebecca and I have discussed this and prayed about this Hope I love you and although Robin will always be my first love. I would be very happy if you would be my wife." Hope was not expecting this at all. Robert continued, "I would like to be a father to Bobbi and Rebecca would like you to be her mother, since she never had a mother."

Hope was crying, Robert said, "Why are you crying, don't you want to marry me?" Hope said, "I'm crying because I wasn't expecting this." After a few minutes, Hope said, "I would very much like to be your wife." Rebecca and Bobbi said, "We going to be sisters, I always wanted to have a sister. They both laughed and hugged each other.

Rebecca said, "There are four bedrooms so we can share a room or you can have your own if you want."

Hope said," I can use one bedroom for a sewing room; I make Bobbi's and my clothes. I can make yours to Rebecca. I don't make all the clothes just some of them."

Rebecca said, "I would like that mom. Is it alright to call you that?" Hope said, "Yes you can." Robert said, "Bobbi you can call me dad if you want." Bobbi said, "Thanks, I think I will."

Hope was so excited about getting married again. She had a lot on her mind. Hope had to contact her parents to tell them that she was getting married. A few days later Hope and Bobbi had gone over to Robert's house to talk about the wedding.

Hope said, "I would like to make my own wedding dress and dresses for the girls." Robert said, "That would be a lot of work. Are you sure that you will have time with everything else have to do before the wedding?" Hope said, "Yes, I never had a real wedding. We went to the courthouse and got married by the judge. We didn't have a lot of money we just had a few friends and family there."

Hope continued, "Now that I teaching fulltime I can afford to do the things that I couldn't do before."

The happy couple set the wedding date, December 20th. Hope said, "I always wanted a Christmas wedding." Robert said, "Are you sure, as you know it gets very cold and we can get a foot of snow." Hope said, I know, but I love Christmas I always have ever since I was a little girl."

Robert said, "OK, you win we can have a Christmas wedding." Hope said, "Thank You." Robert said, "You're Welcome."

Hope made a beautiful wedding dress with a lot of lace and beads and puffy sleeves. Rebecca and Bobbi each had a red velvet dress with puffy sleeves. Robert wore a black tux with a red tie and a white shirt. Robert had asked David to be his best man. Hope didn't have any sisters so she asked Danielle to be her Maid of Honor. Hope had made Danielle's dress too. Robert and Hope went overseas on their honeymoon; before they went they took the girls to Phoenix to grandma and grandpa's house. Bobbi was excited to meet her new grandparents.

While in Phoenix grandma and grandpa took the girls sightseeing. This wasn't new for Rebecca because she had seen all of this before; she was excited to see the excitement in Bobbi's face since this it was all new to her.

When everyone got back home there was a lot to do. They moved a lot of Hope and Bobbi's things to Robert's house. In the process of moving Robert had mentioned that he would like to adopt Bobbi and have her name legally changed to Jackson.

After dinner that night Robert had said, "Bobbi I would like to talk to you about something." Bobbi looked worried. Dad did I do something wrong?" Robert said, "No, your mom and I were talking and I would like to adopt you and have to legally be my daughter, would you like that?" Bobbi said, "I would love that. I wanted that more than anything but I was afraid that you wouldn't want me to have your name. Robert said, "Why wouldn't you think that I love you just as much as Rebecca. I would very much like you to be my daughter."

Bobbi said, "Yes, I love you too. I was just thinking about dad and how I miss him. I didn't want him to go away." Robert said, I understand, I know how you feel. I felt the same way when Robin died."

The whole family went to the adoption agency to get the proceedings started. The agent had given Robert papers to sign. The agent looked everything over then said, "Everything looks good, I will send the papers into the state and the state will have the papers notarized. You should get the papers in a couple of months, maybe sooner it is hard to say. Everything will be sent by certified mail."

Robert said, "Thank You for everything, you have been very helpful. The agent said, "You're Welcome and good luck." Robert said, "This calls for a celebration; let's have lunch and then a maybe a movie. Where do you want to eat?" Bobbi said, "I don't care where we eat, just as long as it's nice." Rebecca said, "I like Chinese, can we go there?" Robert said, "We can, it's been a long time since we had Chinese, right Rebecca?" Rebecca said, "Right dad." Robert said, "Is Chinese alright with you Hope." Hope said, "Bobbi and I never had Chinese before but we are willing to try anything at least once."

Rebecca was practicing every day for the big race that was coming up in a few weeks. With the wedding and visiting grandma and grandpa, Rebecca didn't have much time to practice.

At the race Rebecca won. When Rebecca went up to accept the trophy and check she was surprised to see her grandparents. Her grandparents said, "We wanted to surprise you." Rebecca said, "You did, how long can you stay" Grandma said, "We sold the house and we decided to move to Iowa to be closer to family."

Rebecca said, "That's great, I was hoping that you would move here. I always wanted you to move here when we did." Grandpa said, "We talked about it for a long time but we couldn't decide when we should make the big change."

Grandma and Grandpa adjusted well to the climate and weather change, it was very different from Phoenix. Robert found a nice little house in town for his parents.

Rebecca's grandparents went to all Rebecca's competitions. They were very proud of her achievements.

After Robert and Hope were married a few short months Hope had not been feeling well, she had an idea what it could be but that was impossible. Hope had been married several years before having Bobbi and she wasn't married that long.

Hope went to the doctor for a checkup, the doctor said, "Hope how long have you been feeling this way?" Hope said, "Not long maybe a few weeks why?" The doctor said, "Hope, you're pregnant."

Hope couldn't wait to get home and tell Robert. When she got home, Robert was in his office working. Hope didn't want to bother him while he was working. Hope went in to say that she was home. Robert said, "Hi, you're home already, how was your day?"

Hope said, "It was fine, I'll tell you about it later. I am going to get dinner started. Where are the girls?" Robert said, "In their room doing homework."

After dinner Hope said, "I have something I need to say to all of you." Robert said, "We're all listening." Hope said, "After school today I went to the doctor. He told me something that I had suspected but I wasn't positive. I'm pregnant." All three said, "You're pregnant!" Hope said, "Yes, sometime after the first of the year." I am going to talk to the school board to get a year off from teaching to take care of the baby."

Everyone was excited to have a little one around the house. Hope was busy making little booties and blankets. Robert needed to make room in the sewing room for the crib and all the rest of the baby furniture. Robert said, "Hope we need to move your sewing room downstairs in the room next to the kitchen." Hope said that was fine. "We should have made that room my sewing room when we first moved here."

Hope continued, "You had a hard time getting everything up the stairs. Now, you have to bring everything down again." Robert said, "I don't mind it wasn't that hard."

Hope was glad she had asked for a leave of absence from her job. She had forgotten how tiring being pregnant was. But then she was quite a bit younger when she had Bobbi too.

The day finally came, in February Hope gave birth to a healthy baby boy; they named him John Robert, J.R. for short. Hope was very busy taking care of J.R. Even though Robert was home to help there were still a lot of things to do. Laundry was the biggest chore but Hope loved every bit of it."

The Spencer family came over a couple weeks later they wanted to adjust with having a new addition to the family.

A few years later Rebecca had started college and Danny was in his senior year. Danny had started going out on runs with his dad, he wanted to eventually take over the business.

Danny and Rebecca were becoming more than friends, Danny had asked Rebecca out to a movie or to dinner. Danny was having feelings for Rebecca and wanted to spend the rest of his life with Rebecca.

One night after dinner Danny was very quiet. David asked, "Danny are you o.k. is anything wrong?" Danny said, "No, I just have a lot on my mind." David said, "Would you like to talk about it?" Danny said, "I love Rebecca and I have to talk to Robert because I want to marry Rebecca and I don't know how to approach Robert."

Danny continued, "I just need to pray and ask God for the right words. I am going to my room, night dad. See you in the morning." David said, "Night son."

The next day Danny didn't have any morning classes so he decided to talk to Robert. Robert said, "Hi Danny, Rebecca isn't here she had morning classes today." Danny said, "I know I came to talk to you, is there somewhere where we can talk privately?"

Robert said, "Yes, we can go to my office." Robert continued, "What can I do for you." Danny said, "I have been praying about this for a while, I don't know where to start." Robert waited. Danny continued, "As you know I love Rebecca and I would like to marry her with your permission of course."

Robert said, "I know you love Rebecca and you may have her hand in marriage and after the marriage you can have everything else. Welcome to the family son." Danny said, "Thank you sir."

Now I need to ask Rebecca, I hope she will have me." Robert said, "If Rebecca loves you enough she will."

The big day was approaching fast and Hope said, "Rebecca I will make your dress if you want." Rebecca said, "Thanks Hope, but dad told me that Grandma kept mom's wedding dress and I want to wear her dress. That way mom can be part of the wedding."

Hope said, "I didn't know that your grandparents had saved your mom's wedding dress. Rebecca said, "I didn't know either." Since Robert's parents already lived here, Robin's parents and Samantha came from Phoenix.

Samantha was the Maid of Honor and Bobbi and Debby were the Brides Maids. Right before the wedding Robert came into the Brides room. Robert said, "I am very happy for you, I am also very sad because I am losing my baby girl." Rebecca said, "You're not losing me I will always be there when you need me." Robert said, "Danny is one lucky young man." Rebecca said, "I know, I am a lucky young lady." Robert said, "Yes, you are. You and Danny have been friend since you were 13 and Danny was 15."

Rebecca said, "I wish mom was here to share this special day." Robert said, "I know sweetheart so do I but she is here in spirit. That's why Grandma thought it would be nice to have you wear your mom's dress. I think we should have Samantha come back in so you can finish getting ready."

Danny and Rebecca had a beautiful wedding. Rebecca loved pastel colors. Rebecca had a summer wedding unlike her dad and Hope. Rebecca chooses lavender for Samantha and yellow and mint green for Debby and Bobbi. They all had matching shoes.

Rebecca's mom's wedding dress a long flowing train and a lot of sequins. Rebecca wore a tiara with a veil covering it.

The happy couple lived with David and Danielle until they found a house. Danny found out that the biggest house in town was going to be torn down because it was so big that no one wanted to buy such big house. The family who had lived there had a big family, now the place is rundown and needed a lot of work.

Danny asked if he could buy it. The answer was why, what would you do with it. Danny said, "My wife and I want to fix it up and turn it into a boarding house for homeless people or anyone who needs a place to stay."

Danny was quoted a price and he accepted the offer. The house had 7 bedrooms a huge kitchen and big living and dining room both with a fireplace. The huge backyard had a garden there was enough room to add on when they started a family.

The whole family pitched in to clean inside and outside. After the house was moving in ready, Samantha had told Rebecca that she wasn't going to go back to Phoenix. Rebecca said, "Why" Samantha said, "I like it here and I want to help with running this boarding house of yours." Rebecca said, "I'm glad you like it here and we will need all the help we can get."

The town council put up signs by the main road and the highway leading into town advertising the boarding house and that they were open for business. The signs read "Spencer's boarding house" and under the name it said, "Your home away from home."

HOME AWAY FROM HOME

MAIN CHARACTERS 2

Danny Spencer	—	Vet like his father and owner of the boardinghouse
Rebecca Spencer	—	Danny's wife
Joy Marie Spencer	—	Danny and Rebecca's daughter
Ruth Ann Spencer & Robin Jo Spencer	—	Danny and Rebecca's twin daughters
Shaun Jones	—	a boarder at the boardinghouse
April Steven's	—	a boarder at the boardinghouse
Colin Steven's-Jones	—	Shaun and April's son
Shaun Matthew& Scott Joseph	—	Shaun and April's twin sons
Barbara (Bobbi) Powell	—	Rebecca's sister
James & John Powell	—	Bobbi's twin sons

HOME AWAY FROM HOME

DANNY AND REBECCA PRAYED that the boarding house would be a big success. One of the boarders was a gentleman by the name of Shaun Jones. Shaun showed up on the Spencer's doorstep with only the clothes on his back.

Danny asked, "How can I help you?" Shaun said, "I saw your sign, I have been out of work and living on the streets for a while now and I need a place to stay."

Danny said, "Please come in, have a seat in the living room. Tell me about yourself. Why are you living on the street?" Shaun said, "I lost my job." Danny asked, "What did you do, for a job I mean?"

Shaun told Danny, "I worked in factory and the business moved. We were told we could move but my roots are here and didn't want to move." Danny asked, "Have you looked for work?" Shaun said, "I got jobs here and there. Nothing permanent though."

Danny said, "We have only lived here a short time and there is a lot of work to do to fix up this old house. I could pay you to help fix it up. I can't pay much but it will help you get started." Shaun said, "Thank you."

Another person was a young 17 year old young lady that was pregnant, her name was April Stevens. Her parents had asked her to leave when they found out that she was pregnant, they had told her that they were not happy with her present situation and said that they couldn't afford to have another mouth to feed.

April asked, "Rebecca can I take some on line classes." Rebecca asked, "What kind of classes do you have in mind?" April said, "I'm not sure, I thought maybe a typing class or something like that. I always wanted to be a secretary."

After talking to Danny Rebecca told April that they would pay for her classes in exchange for her room and board. After getting a job April agreed to pay Danny and Rebecca the money that was owed to them for the classes.

One day Rebecca had stopped by her dad's house for a visit. Her dad said, "Why don't you go out to see Sampson? He misses you?" Rebecca said, "I think I will but I don't have time to ride anymore." Rebecca went out to the barn. She went up to Sampson and said, "I missed you and I will come and visit more often." Sampson nudged her because he knew that she had treats in her pocket. Rebecca laughed Sampson you know me to well. Bye Sampson, I will come and visit you soon. Sampson just snickered like he understood her.

Danny and Rebecca had also set up a soup kitchen. That way they can feed the homeless on Holidays. Danny said, "I didn't realize that there were so many homeless people. I think we should do the soup kitchen more often." Rebecca said, "I agree, maybe we should do this every week. That way they will have a good hot meal at least once a week. Thank you for suggesting it." Danny said, "You're Welcome."

Danny and Rebecca were married a little over a year when Rebecca realized that she was pregnant. April was close to her due date only a couple of months away. Rebecca was about three months along.

Robert, Hope, David and Danielle were thrilled with the news that they were going to be grandparents. Hope and Danielle had a baby shower for Rebecca; they also agreed to have a baby shower for April too.

April said, "Why are you having a shower for me, I'm not family?" Rebecca said, "I asked Hope and Danielle if they would include you because you are family and so is Shaun. You don't have to be family to give a baby shower to someone."

Rebecca continued, "Have you talked to your mom lately? "April said, "I talked to her but she doesn't want me to move back." She said, "You made a mistake and I tried to talk you into making the mistake to go away but you didn't listen. Now you have to live with the mistake for the rest of life."

Rebecca said, "What about the father what does he has to say." April said, "We were careless and when I told him I was pregnant, he dumped me like a hot potato. He said that it was all my doing that I pressured him into it. He didn't believe me when I told him that it wasn't true." Hope asked, "Where did you live when you left your parent's home?" April said, "Just like Shaun, I was living on the streets for a while. After that I just walking and ended up here, I felt that nobody loved me and that I was all alone."

Hope said, "You are not alone. We all love you and someone else loves you." April said, "Who would that be?" Hope said, "God loves you he will never leave you. We will be here whenever you need us."

April said, "Rebecca had asked me to go with them to church, but I told her that I had things to do. Then I would sit in my room and feel sorry for myself and cry." April continued "Will you forgive me for lying." Rebecca said, "I knew in time when you would tell me. I forgive you and so does God." Danielle said, "We have a bible study and we would be happy to have you." April said, "I would like that. I would like to go to church too." Hope said, "We would love to have you. You will like Pastor Joe and his wife Carrie. They used to come to the bible study but not as much as before. They have grandchildren now and they want to help their children all they can."

On Sunday Shaun and April went to church with Danny and Rebecca. They both thought that Pastor Joe and Carrie were very nice. Shaun didn't go to church either.

April was doing very well in her typing class. April found a job at the insurance company in town. April told them that she was going to have a baby in a few weeks. The agency told her that it would not be a problem.

April had given birth to a boy she named him Colin Michael. A few months later Rebecca gave birth to a girl they named her Joy Marie. Danny and Rebecca named her Joy because she was the Joy of their lives. April had turned 18 a few months after Colin was born. Shaun had feelings for April but he never showed them before. One night after dinner, Shaun said, "April I have something very important to ask you." April said, "What did you want to ask me?"

Shaun said, "I don't know if you noticed, but I have wanted to ask you out for a long time.

Shaun continued, "I would like to marry you and be a father to Colin." April said, "I don't know what to say. I don't know if I'm ready to get married. I am just getting used to being a mother. I don't know if I am ready to be a wife too." Shaun said, "I understand I know this is a big adjustment for you and you need time to sort things out."

April said, "I won't get married to someone just to have a father for my baby. I need time to pray about it.?" Shaun said, "I will never ask you to do that." April said, "Do what." Shaun said, "To marry someone just to marry him for the sake of a baby. I love you and I want to marry you, and I will love Colin like he was my own." April said, "Colin will be yours if we do get married. I know that my ex-boyfriend doesn't want to have anything to do with me or Colin. I called mom and dad about Colin and they wanted to see him but that was all they said except that Tom was serious about someone and they were getting married, but they didn't say when."

Shaun said, "Are you saying that you will marry me?" April said, "I'm not sure yet. I will have to think more about it. All I can say is all you will get right now is a maybe."

April was in the kitchen getting something to eat. Rebecca walked in and said, "April are you ok, or is something wrong with Colin?" April said, "We are both fine, why." Rebecca said, "You just seem that you are preoccupied about something. Do you want to talk?" April said, "Shaun told me that he had feelings for me and that he wanted to be a father to Colin." Rebecca said, "What did you tell him?" April said, "I told him that I was just getting used to being a mother and that I wasn't sure if I was ready to be a wife too. Also I didn't want anyone to marry me just for the sake of a baby. Shaun said that he wouldn't do that?" Rebecca said "Do what." April said, "That what I said. He said I wouldn't marry anyone just because of a baby, he also said that he loved me and that he would love Colin as if he were his own." Rebecca said, "What did you tell him?" Are going to marry Shaun?" April said, "I don't know I haven't given him an answer yet."

Rebecca asked, "Do you love Shaun, enough to marry him?" April said, "I never thought about it. I know that he would be a great father." Rebecca said, "Why don't you pray about it. God will give you the right words."

That night April prayed, God I am very new at praying. I do love Shaun, I know that he will be a good father and he does love Colin. Just give me the right words to say when I talk to Shaun. Amen."

A couple of days later April found Shaun reading the newspaper. April said, "Shaun I would like to talk to you if you're not busy." Shaun put the paper down and said, "I'm not busy, just reading the paper. What would you talk about?" April said, "I have been thinking and praying about what you asked him the other day." Shaun said, "And, what did you decide?" April said, "I know you love me and Colin, I love you too and I would love to spend the rest of my life with you."

Shaun asked, "Would you like to move or would you like to live here?" April said, "For now I would like to live here if you don't mind." Shaun said, "I don't mind, I like it here too."

April and Rebecca had a lot to do before the wedding. April didn't have many friends. She did ask her parents to come to the wedding. Her parents agreed to come. April was surprised; she didn't think they would come, since they had problems in the past. Shaun didn't have many friends or family close by so he asked Danny to be his best man. April had asked Rebecca to be her Maid of Honor. April and Shaun had wanted a small wedding, they weren't fancy people so they didn't want a fancy wedding.

April and Shaun didn't go on a honeymoon. April had gone back to work since she had taken off to have the baby. Shaun loved to bake. He had gotten a job at the local bakery. They had planned on going on a trip later on when Colin was a little older, and he would be easier to take care of.

Rebecca asked, "April do you know how to ride?" April asked, "Ride what." Rebecca said, "Sorry, do you know how to ride a horse?" April said, "No" Rebecca said, "I was competing in barrel races since I was 14. Now I don't ride much anymore."

April said, "Do you miss it?" Rebecca said, "I do miss it but I don't have the time now with the baby and everything." Rebecca continued, "Danny was my teacher. I knew how to ride but barrel riding is different." April said, "Do you want to ride again?" Rebecca said, "Not barrel riding but I miss riding Sampson. I had a horse Cinnamon that I loved very much. Dad and I brought her with us when we moved here." April asked, "What happened to Cinnamon?" Rebecca said, "One day it was winter time and Samantha and I were riding in the woods not far from the Spencer home. It was very icy and there was a patch of ice on the path and I didn't see it. I fell and Cinnamon fell, I asked Samantha to go get David, he was a vet and he would know what to do.?" April said, "What happened?" Rebecca said, "David came I had broken my arm but Cinnamon had a broken leg and David had to put her down. She is buried on the path under the tree near the waterfall."

April said, "Do you ever go to the waterfall?" Rebecca said "No, but I did go to dad's a couple of weeks ago to see Sampson. I got him after Cinnamon died. I rode him in the barrel races. I will teach you how to ride if you want to learn." April said, "I want to learn but I don't know what to do with Colin." Rebecca said, "Hope and dad will take care of him, I am bringing Joy too." Hope said she misses having babies in the house. There hasn't been a baby in the house since J.R. was born. Now she has fun with grandchildren. April said, "Is Joy their only grandchild." Rebecca said, "No, Her daughter Bobbi has Twin boys." April said, "I didn't know that Hope had other children, I just assumed that Bobbi was your dad's and Hope's." Rebecca said, "Hope was married before just like dad was. When dad married Hope he adopted Bobbi as his child. Dad and Hope had so much in common both of their spouses died."

April and Rebecca went to her dad's house with babies in tow. Rebecca had taken April to the place where Cinnamon was buried. April said, "It's so beautiful here, it like a little piece of Heaven. I have never seen Heaven of course but I can imagine this is what Heaven might look like." Rebecca said, "I thought the same thing when I first saw this place."

After their ride they decided to visit David and Danielle before going to pick up the children. David said, "Rebecca what a surprise. Where is my granddaughter?" Rebecca said, "April and I went riding and we left the babies at dad's."

Rebecca continued, "I promise to bring Joy over real soon." Danielle said, "Would you like some cookies before you go, I made your favorite," Rebecca said, "Danielle you spoil me. I appreciate it but we can't stay, we told Hope we wouldn't be gone long. Hope told me that we didn't have to hurry, they both loved to have the children. Danielle said, "Then please stay we miss you. We don't see you or Danny anymore."

Rebecca said, "I know Danny has been busy working and I have busy taking care of Joy and keeping the house clean."

David said, "April how do you like being married?" April said, "I love being married. At first I wasn't sure what to expect." David said "Meaning what?" April said, "Well, most people get married first and then have children, not the other way around. I am just getting used to being married." Rebecca said, "Thanks for the cookies but we really need to go. Danny and Shaun will be home soon and I need to get dinner started." Danielle said, "You're welcome, please come back when you can stay longer." Rebecca said, "I promise I will bring Joy and if Danny can make it I will bring him too." Danielle said, "April you and Shaun can come anytime. April said, "Thanks for the offer."

When Rebecca and April got home they put the babies down for their nap. April said, "I can't believe how tired I am." Rebecca commented, "You will be very sore for a day or two, you are not used to being on a horse."

When Shaun got home from work he asked April, "How was your day." April said, "It was fine." Shaun asked, "What did you do today." April said, "Rebecca and I went to her dad's house and left the children there and then we went horseback riding and then stopped in and visited with David and Danielle."

Shaun said, "I guess you were busy today." April said, "I was, and now I am tired. Rebecca said that I would be sore for a couple of days because I was never on a horse before, and we did ride a long time."

A few days later the weekly bible study was at the Spencer household. April and Shaun had been talking. When the bible study was almost over Shaun said, "April and I would like to know what we need to do to be members of the church and we want to be baptized too." Robert said, "When Rebecca and I became members and were baptized, Pastor Joe had a class explaining what baptism means." Rebecca continued by saying," Pastor Joe does these classes for everyone."

April said, "Does Pastor Joe baptize babies." Rebecca said, "No, some Pastors do have water baptism for infants, but our church doesn't do that."

Shaun said, "That's O.K. we were just asking." On Sunday April and Shaun talked to Pastor Joe about the classes, and when it was time to be baptized the congregation met at the lake not far from the church." They usually have the baptism at the lake. The Pastor said, "We need to add on to the church. The church isn't big enough to hold a baptismal font."

The congregation agreed. "We can hold a fund raiser of some kind." Someone asked. Pastor Joe said, "That's good idea, what did you have in mind." "We could have a carnival with rides games that sort of thing." Someone had said. Pastor Joe said, "We can have it in the field across from the church."

The carnival was a huge success. They hadn't raised enough money to add on. After some prayer, one of the members had mentioned that they had received some money from a relative that had passed away. The family wanted to give a portion of it to the church.

Pastor Joe couldn't believe that someone would do that. He had prayed that God would find another way to raise money. They were short thousands of dollars.

As the years went by April's family grew and so did Rebecca's. April and Shaun had moved out of the boarding house. Shaun wanted to stay in town so they moved to a nice two story house. After Colin was born, April gave birth to twin boys a year later. April and Shaun named them Shaun Matthew and Scott Joseph.

About the same time Rebecca gave birth to twin girls. Rebecca and Danny named them Ruth Ann and Robin Jo. Danny had talked to his dad and Shaun about adding on to the boarding house. The house had several bedrooms already, but if they wanted to take in more boarders then they would need more bedrooms.

There were five bedrooms already, Shaun had one bedroom and April had one room. After the wedding April moved into Shaun's room and when Colin was born then he was in April's old room.

After the Jones family moved out Joy, moved out of her parent's bedroom and into Shaun's old room and when the twins were born they took April's old room. Samantha had gotten married and moved out. That left two bedrooms for boarders. The bedrooms were empty right now since there were no boarders at the moment, but that could change at any time.

Shaun and David agreed to help in building the extra bedrooms. Since the Spencer family was complete they agreed to add on two more bedrooms upstairs and a playroom for the girls downstairs.

April had talked to Rebecca about riding lessons for Colin April wanted him to learn. The twins were still too young. Rebecca said, "I will talk to dad and see if he would teach Colin. I would like Joy to learn too, I just don't have the time to teach them. April said, "Thanks, I would appreciate it." April continued, "I don't have the time to teach them either, I thought it would be better for you to ask than for me to ask."

Robert agreed to teach Colin and his granddaughter. Robert said, "I will pick them up Saturday morning around 9:00, then maybe you and April can come for lunch." Rebecca said, "I will be there, I'm sure April will come too but I will ask her. I f she doesn't then I will take the Colin home."

Robert asked, "How is Danny, I haven't seen him for a while." Rebecca said, "He's fine, he has been very busy working." Rebecca continued, "He has been working too hard and I am worried about him."

Robert said, "Why are you worried." Rebecca said, "He comes home and he is so tired I'm afraid that he will get sick." Robert said, "Have you been praying." Rebecca said, "Yes, I know that God will keep him safe, but I still worry."

Later that day Rebecca called Danielle. Rebecca said, "Is it all right if I come over." Danielle said, "You don't have to ask you can come over anytime." When Rebecca arrived Danielle sensed that something was wrong. Danielle asked, "What's wrong is everything alright?" Rebecca said, "Everything is fine, I just want to talk." Danielle said, "Ok what about."

Rebecca said, "When David was a vet was David tired a lot and run down?" Danielle said, "Sometimes when he got a call in the middle of the night, why do you ask?" Rebecca said, "Sometimes Danny comes home and he is so tired that he misses dinner, I can't always wake him up to eat. When I ask if he is ok, he says he's fine. I am worried that he will get sick and I won't be able to take care of him."

Danielle said, "The weather hasn't been the best either, since we have been having such a strange winter and spring, the temperature has been up in down, I'm surprised that people are not all sick."

Rebecca said, "I know that's why I'm worried about him. I told dad that I have been praying I know that God will keep him safe." Danielle said, "Keep me posted, David and I will be praying too." Rebecca said, "I will."

When Rebecca got home she noticed that Danny's truck was in the driveway. She was glad to have him home at a normal hour. When she walked into the house it was very quiet. Rebecca said, "Danny? He didn't answer. Rebecca repeated, "Danny." She walked through the house, and she found him in the bedroom asleep. Rebecca thought that was strange because when he takes a nap he falls asleep in the chair or on the couch. Rebecca went over to check on him, Danny was very warm, and Rebecca was afraid something like this was going to happen. Rebecca said, "Danny, Danny woke up, and said, "I am so cold do we have any more blankets." Rebecca said, "Yes, I'll get them." When she came back Danny was asleep again. So she covered him up with another blanket and kissed him on the forehead and left the room.

Rebecca called Danielle. Rebecca said, "I just wanted to let you know that when I got home Danny was home and he is sick. I found him in bed asleep. When he woke up he said, he was cold and asked for a blanket, when I came back he was asleep again. Can you go to school and pick up the girls? I don't want to leave, in case Danny wakes up and needs something."

Danielle said I'll leave right now." Rebecca said, "Thanks." Danielle said, "You're welcome."

When Danielle dropped the girls off she asked, "How's Danny?" Rebecca said, "I just checked on him, he's asleep." Danielle said, "Sleep is the best thing right now. Call if you need anything,"

After Danielle left, Danny woke up and asked, "Who was here I thought I heard voices." Rebecca said, "You did, I called your mom, she went to pick up the girls from school. How are you feeling?" Danny said, "I am so tired." Rebecca said "You're sick, that's why, and you need all the sleep you can get."

Danny said, "I need to get up I need to work so I can provide for my family." Rebecca said, "You're mom told me that your dad will take over the vet patients until you're on your feet again, so you stay put." Rebecca continued, "Are you hungry would you like some soup?" Danny said, "Not now maybe later." Rebecca said," ok, I'll come back later."

After a few days Danny was feeling better but wasn't up to going to work yet. Danny was grateful that his dad took over as vet. David and Danielle came over to the house to see how Danny was feeling. David asked, "How are you feeling?" Danny said, "I'm fine but I still get tired real easy, I want to thank you also for taking over the vet business for me." David said, "No problem, I was glad to do it. I miss taking care of animals." Danielle asked, "What did the doctor say?" Rebecca said, "Not much, all he said was with the change of weather and Danny working too hard he needed to take better care of himself. Rest was the best thing to make him slow down."

A few days later Danny was back to work. He promised Rebecca that he would take it easy and to stay warm.

Rebecca was surprised when Bobbi called. Rebecca hadn't talked to her in a while. Bobbi said, "I need someone to talk to I don't know what to do."

Rebecca said, "Bobbi what's wrong." Bobbi said, "As you know, Kevin turned away from God, I tried to talk to him and start coming back to church with me and the kids." Bobbi continued, "We had a fight because I found out by accident that he was cheating on me. He is gone a lot on business and I found a phone number in his pants pocket. I asked Kevin about it and he said it was a business associate. I called the number and a child answered, so I know he was lying to me. I questioned Kevin again and he admitted that he had been with another woman."

Rebecca said, "Does this woman know about you?" Bobbi said, "I'm not sure, I hung up when that little boy answered the phone."

Rebecca said, "Did you talk to mom and dad yet." Bobbi said, "No, I tried but no one answered, then I called you." Rebecca said, "Why don't you pack up the kids and come home. We all miss you and I'm sure Danny won't mind you coming to stay with us. I know mom and dad would want you stay with them too."

Bobbi said, "I was hoping you would say that but I didn't want to sound pushy." Rebecca said, "You're not pushy you're family and families stick together." Bobbi said, "Thanks, we will get there as soon as we can."

When Bobbi got to Rebecca's house she hugged Rebecca and said hi to Danny. Bobbi said, "I can't believe I am here I missed you. I can't get over how big the girls are. I seems that they were just babies not too long ago."

Rebecca said, "I know what you mean, they grow up so fast." After everyone was settled Rebecca called her parents and told them the situation and that Bobbi and the kids were here. Hope said, "We will be over soon, how is she." Rebecca said, "She's a mess she was in tears when she got here. She said that she doesn't know what to do. She still loves him and hates him at the same time." Bobbi said, "Is that mom I want to talk to her." Rebecca said, "Just a minute mom," Its mom her and dad will be right over. Rebecca said, "Bobbi wanted to know if I was talking to you." Rebecca continued, "Bye mom see you soon."

When Hope and Robert got there Bobbi hugged them and cried on her mom's shoulder. Hope said, "Bobbi have you talked to Kevin." Bobbi said, "Yes, I tried talking to him and tried reasoning with him. I asked him why he was doing this to us and if he still loved us. Hope said, "What did he say." Bobbi said, "He couldn't give me a yes or no answer." Robert said, "That's not an answer either he loves you or he doesn't."

Hope said, "What are you going to do." Bobbi said, "I don't know yet. I am just going to pray and ask God." Robert said, "We'd love you to come home and stay with us while you sort things out. Bobbi said, "Thanks but I want to stay here for a day or two and visit with Rebecca. Then I will come and stay at the house. Maybe I will go riding while I'm here." Maybe I might even go and visit David and Danielle too. Danny said, "They would love to see you." Bobbi said, "How is Debby, is she living around here." Danny said, "No, I guess there was no way you would have known, but Debby had a stroke about three years ago and she lives in a nursing home in Davenport." Bobbi said, "I didn't know, I'm sorry. Can I go and see her." Rebecca said, "Yes, we can go tomorrow if you want." Bobbi said, Yes, I would like that." Rebecca said, "We can leave right after breakfast Danny can get Joy off to school we should be back in time to get Ruth and Robin off to preschool." The boys asked, "Can we stay here with Uncle Danny or do we have to go along."

Danny said, "You can stay here if you want too. If I get a call while you're gone than I will leave a note saying that I took them to your mom's.

The boys said, "Can we mom." Bobbi said, since Danny said that it's ok, and then it's ok with me."

The next day Rebecca and Bobbi left for Davenport to see Debby. Rebecca said, "Don't be surprised if Debby doesn't recognize you. You have been gone a long time. We get here at least once a week sometimes two it depends on if we have errands to do or if Debby has a bad day, the nurse's call us or Danielle daily to give us updates on how she is doing."

After visiting Debby Rebecca and Bobbi stopped at the mall and did some shopping and then headed for home. Bobbi said, "That was fun, I missed that girl talk we used to have." Rebecca said, "I missed the girl talk too." Danny was home when they got back. Danny asked, "How's Debby today?" Rebecca said, "She's fine, I told Bobbi that she might not recognize her, but Debby did remember her and we had a good visit." Danny said, "That's good you had a good time." Rebecca said, "Have you had lunch yet." Danny said, "No, I was just going to make the boys and myself something when you drove up."

Rebecca said, "I will make lunch then." Bobbi asked, "What did you and Uncle Danny do today." James said, "We helped with the yard work." John said, "Danny let us mow the lawn and trim the bushes." James said, "We did a good job and he even gave us each $5.00." Bobbi said, "Danny you shouldn't have done that." Danny said, "Why not, I always pay my workers if they do a good job."

The next day Bobbi, Rebecca, and the boys went to Grandma and Grandpa Jackson's house to go riding. Rebecca asked April if they wanted to join them. April said, "That the twins were sick but Colin wanted to come." Rebecca said, "She would pick Colin up on the way."

James asked, "Who is Colin?" Rebecca said, "Colin's mom April and his dad Shaun were our first boarders when we bought the house. Shaun Jr. and Scott are their twin boys."

John asked, "How older is Colin?" Rebecca said, "Colin is 8 the same age as Joy. Shaun and Scott are 6 the same age as Ruth and Robin." Rebecca continued, "It's Ironic that both times our babies were born a few months of each other." James asked, "What does ironic mean." Rebecca said, "It's means strange" John said, "Then why didn't you just say that." Rebecca laughed, "I don't know, it just came out."

After the horseback riding Bobbi and the boys stayed at mom and dads. The boys liked visiting their grandparents; they wanted to stay with Rebecca and Danny. Bobbi said, "No, grandma has more room since Rebecca just got new boarders." Rebecca said, "You can visit anytime though."

Bobbi decided to stay instead of going back to her husband. She found a nice house not far from Rebecca and Danny. Since Bobbi was staying she had to find a job and enroll the boys in school. Since the end of the school year was almost here, Bobbi didn't have much time to get the boys signed up for school.

Bobbi also found out that there was an opening for a teacher. Bobbi said, "I never went to school for teaching. I went to college but I never took any teaching classes." The school board said, "Would you be willing to take night classes to get your teaching degree." Bobbi said, "I would be willing to do that." The school board said, "Good, we are very happy to have you on our staff Mrs. Powell." Bobbi said, "Thank you, but please call me Bobbi or Ms. Curtis, I am in the process of divorcing my husband, my children will be going to school here and I don't want any confusion or having other children think I give James and John special attention because they are my children."

One of the school board members said, "We understand, Bobbi. Will you be able to find someone to watch the boys while you are in school." Bobbi said, "Yes, that won't be a problem. My sister lives here and so do my parents."

When Bobbi got to Rebecca's to pick up the boys. Rebecca said, "What took you so long, I thought you were only going to enroll the boys." Bobbi said, "That was the plan but when I arrived I found out that there was an opening for a teacher. The school board asked if I was interested, I told them that I went to college but not for teaching. One of the members said that I could go to school at night. So would you be willing to take care of the boys, while I'm in school."

Rebecca said, "We would love to have the boys, how many days a week will it be." Bobbi said "I forgot to ask, is it going to be a problem." Rebecca said, "No, I was just wondering."

Bobbi was very busy with teaching school and going to school three nights a week. She was grateful that that Rebecca took care of the boys. She dropped the boys off after supper and then picked them up around 9:00.

When Bobbi picked the boys up Rebecca said, "Bobbi you look so tired. How long before you are done with your classes." Bobbi said, "I am tired, I am almost done with the first semester. Then there is a break for Christmas. I think I will sleep the whole vacation away." Rebecca just looked at her and laughed.

Now that the church added on Pastor Joe thanked everyone for their help. Now we can have baptism classes year round. Shaun and April were ready to have their children baptized. Danny and Rebecca were ready too. Bobbi's children were already baptized. Pastor Joe had told the congregation that they will have the classes starting next week.

Bobbi finished her night classes and received her teaching degree. Everyone was very proud of her. Robert said, "This calls for a celebration." Bobbi said, "Don't go through all that fuss. I don't need a party." Hope said, "Nonsense not every day my daughter gets her teaching degree. My parents gave me a party.

After a few weeks after the party Bobbi had gotten a notice in the mail that her divorce was final and all she had to do was sign papers. She looked for the papers in the packet that came in the mail. She called her lawyer. The lawyer said, "Bobbi you need to come here to fill them out." Bobbi said, "I have a job I can't just pick up and leave. Why can't you just send they and I can mail them and I will send them back?" The lawyer said, "Your husband claims that he still loves you and wants you and the children to come back. He said he wants you to give him another chance." Bobbi said, "He had his chance, it's too late. I moved on and he should too. If still wants to see the boys that's fine. I won't be moving back I'm happy here and I plan on staying." Her lawyer said, "I will contact his lawyer and inform him what you said. I will send the papers by express then said them back." Bobbi said, "Thank you."

After taking to her lawyer Bobbi called her mom. Bobbi said, "Mom my lawyer called me and informed me that Kevin wants another chance. He said that he still loves me and wants us to come back home." Hope said, "What did you tell him." Bobbi said, "What do think I told him. I told my lawyer to tell Kevin that I am staying here and that it is too late and that he had his chance. The lawyer told me that he would talk to his lawyer. He said that he would also send the papers for me to sign." Hope said, "Good for you, I knew that Kevin was never good enough for you. I never trusted him from the day you got married. I didn't think it would have taken this long though. I thought he would have shown his true colors before this."

Bobbi said, "Why didn't you tell me that you never trusted him." Hope said, "I never said anything because it was your life and I felt it wasn't my business."

Bobbi said, "I still would have liked to hear what you had to say. Even if I didn't agree I still would have liked to have heard your opinion." Hope said, "Your right I'm sorry." Bobbi said, "You're forgiven."

Summer was almost here and Kevin wanted to see the boys. The boys were old enough to fly to see their father. At first James and John didn't want to go because they never forgave him for the way he treated them and what he did to their mother. After a long conversion Bobbi convinced them that she moved on and they shouldn't hate their dad. Even though she couldn't live with him she still wanted the boys to have a relationship with their dad.

When the James and John got home they had told Bobbi that their dad tried to convince them to live with him. They had told their dad no, they wanted to live where they were living. Bobbi was not happy with what the boys had told them. She said, "Don't worry I will talk to your dad."

Bobbi called Kevin and said, "If you pull anything like this again I will put a restraining order on you and you will never see your kids again." Kevin said, "You can't do that." Bobbi said, "Yes I can, watch me. If you behave yourself I won't do it."

Thanksgiving was just a few days away. Rebecca and Danny invited everyone to their house for Thanksgiving. Rebecca said, "I can't believe that Christmas is just around the corner." Bobbi said, "I can't believe it either. The year went by so fast."

Just like every year Thanksgiving was a time of sharing what they were Thankful for. The family and friends grew every year. I started with David's family and ending with Bobbi's family. Shaun's family had joined them several years ago. Danny and Rebecca had been calling them family, because Shaun was like a brother to them. Rebecca said that April was like a sister to her.

Danny Rebecca and the whole family went to the woods near David's house to cut down there tree. After bring it home the whole family decorated the tree. Rebecca was very quiet. Bobbi asked, "Rebecca is you alright. You seem very quiet?" Rebecca said, "I'm fine, I was just remembering our first Christmas so many years ago. Dad was so sad I know he was missing mom. I miss her too even though I never met her. With all the stories that dad told me about her. I felt like I knew her." Bobbi said, "Do still have her picture?" Rebecca said, "I do, it's on the dresser in our bedroom. I pray to her every night to protect us and to keep us safe."

A few years went by and Shaun and Scott. Ruth and Robin had feelings for each other. They had had known each other since they were babies. All four of them were going to college in the fall.

Shaun and Scott were talking about what they wanted to do with their lives after college. Scott said, "I would like to marry Robin someday." Shaun said, "I would like to marry Ruth too someday." Scott said, "I suppose we will have to talk to Danny to give his permission to ask them." Shaun said, "I never been this nervous. I hope he gives his blessing. I love Ruth I would like to spend the rest of my life with her." Scott said, "I love Robin too."

A few days later Shaun and Scott went to Danny's house. Danny wasn't home he was busy working. Rebecca told them to come in. Rebecca said, "What can I do for you?" Scott said, "We would like to talk to you and Danny." Rebecca said, "Danny should be home soon. Would you like anything to drink while we wait?" Scott said, "No, we will just wait if you don't mind." Rebecca said, "That's fine."

When Danny got home Rebecca told him that we had guests in the living room. Danny said, "Who is it?" Rebecca said, "Scott and Shaun want to talk to us." Danny said, "The last time I heard that. I was asking your dad to marry you."

Danny and Rebecca went into the living room. Danny said, "This is a surprise? What can I do for you?" Scott said, "Shaun and I love your daughters and we would like your permission to marry them after college of course." Danny looked at Rebecca and smiled. Then Danny looked at Scott and Shaun. Danny said, "Permission granted. I will tell you what Robert told me when I asked Rebecca to marry me." They looked at Danny and said, "What was that." Danny said, "He told me I couldn't have picked a better son in law. So I telling you both I couldn't have picked better son in laws than the two of you. Welcome to the family." Shaun and Scott said, "Thank you."

Joy had a boyfriend too. She didn't fall in love with Colin though. She didn't want to be like her sisters and have sisters marry brothers. She had her own identity she wanted to be different. Joy and Chris had set their wedding date for September. Joy had always wanted a fall wedding because it wasn't too cold or too hot.

The day finally arrived and Joy was nervous and excited at the same time. Danny went into the bride's room. Hi honey how are you doing?" Joy said, "I'm alright I think. I didn't think this day would ever come."

After the honeymoon Chris and Joy found a nice three bedroom house in the country. They wanted to get a few horses and maybe a dog or two. Joy loved to ride but Chris never rode before. Joy didn't mind teaching him. She told him that it was easy and there was nothing to it. A few years went by and Joy and Chris had two children. Jacob age two. Paul was six months. Everyone was very happy. The day finally came when Ruth and Robin got married.

Danny and Rebecca couldn't believe that all of their children were married. Danny said, "I am feeling like an old man now." Rebecca said, "I do too. An old woman I mean." Danny said, "I was thinking should we sell the house and move to something smaller." Rebecca said, "Why do you want to do that." Danny said "I was just thinking about it. I am getting too old. I might have to hire someone to do the yard work and other things around the house."

Rebecca said, "I think we should stay here. I don't want to move. If we move where our borders would live, they will have no place to go. I don't want them to go back to living on park benches or cardboard box." Danny said, "You're right I don't want that either."

A few years went by. Scott and Robin had two children both boys. Shaun and Ruth weren't blessed with children yet. Ruth came by one day and talked to her mom. Ruth said, "Mom I'm worried." Rebecca said, "Worried about what." Ruth said, "Well, as you know we have been trying to have a child. We want children so bad. I feel sometimes that God is punishing us for some reason. Rebecca said, "Don't talk like that. God might have something else in mind for you and Shaun." Ruth said, "Like what." Rebecca said, "I don't know, I think you should pray about it and ask God to show you."

Shaun and Ruth prayed and asked for a sign. A few days later they stopped by Rebecca and Danny's. They asked Shaun and April to come over too. Ruth said, "Mom we took your advice. We prayed we have something to say. I don't know how to put this. Shaun and I are moving to Romania and run an orphanage. Now we will have children lots of them. April and Rebecca looked at each other. April said, "Why so far away." Shaun said, "We prayed about it and that is where God wants us to go."

Danny said, "When will you go?" Shaun said, "We plan to leave by the end of summer so we have some time yet."

By the end of summer it was time to say good bye. There were a lot of tears shed. Rebecca said, "We know God wants you to move but we want you to stay here. We will all miss you." Ruth said, "We will miss you too. We will write." Rebecca said, "We will write too." April said, "We will write too."

A couple of days later Robert called Rebecca. Robert asked, "Mom and I were talking and we were wondering if you had any empty rooms or are they all full." Rebecca said, "We have room. Why do ask." Robert said, "We aren't getting any younger and we would like to sell the house and move in with you if you will have us."

Rebecca said, "Dad don't say that of course we will have you. I know Danny won't mind. What will you do with the horses?" Robert said, "I talked to Joy and she said that she will take them."

Robert and Hope sold their house to a lovely couple and moved in with Rebecca and Danny. They were all very happy.